Ladybird

This Little Story

belongs to

Published by Ladybird Books Ltd
27 Wrights Lane London W8 5TZ
A Penguin Company
3 5 7 9 10 8 6 4 2

Printed in Italy

Brave
Little
Train

by Nicola Baxter
illustrated by Toni Goffe

Pht! Pht! Pht! Pht! Phoooooh!

The Station Master shook his head. "I'm sorry," he said. "The Seaside Express simply will not start."

"Oh nooo!" wailed the passengers on the platform, waving their tickets.

"No sandcastles!" cried a boy with four big buckets.

"No paddling!" groaned a businessman with a bushy beard.

"No ice cream!" sniffed the twins.

"I know this is your first long trip," he said, "but remember, all you have to do is follow the track."

"But, but, but… it's a very long way!" spluttered the Little Train.

"You can do it!" said the Station Master, picking up his whistle.

Whoooooooooo! went the whistle.

"Hooraaaaaaaay!" called the passengers.

"Oh… oh… oh… well… here we g-g-go!" puffed the Little Train, and slowly he pulled his three crowded carriages out of the station.

As soon as he was on the open track, the Little Train felt better.

"This, this, this… isn't so bad!" he chuffed quietly to himself.

"We're going to the sea!" yelled the terrible twins.

"It's a very smooth ride!" smiled the lady in blue.

"It's a first class train!" said the businessman with the beard.

"It's fine, fine, fine – if there aren't any hills!" puttered the Little Train under his breath.

But two minutes later...

"Ooooooooooo…er!" yelled the passengers, as they started to climb.

"Help! There goes my hat!" cried the lady in blue.

"Allow me, Madam!" called the businessman with the beard.

"We've caught it with our spades!" screamed the twins together.

"Uphill isn't s-s-so bad – if there isn't any downhill!" puffed the Little Train, red in the face.

But when he got to the top…

"Wheeeeeeeeeeee!" screeched the passengers.

"It's just like the fair!" shouted the boy with the buckets.

"This could blow my beard off!" moaned the man with the whiskers.

"It's almost fun – as long as there are no bridges!" squealed the Little Train as the wind whistled through his wheels.

But just around the corner...

"Aaaaaaaaaaaaaah!" cried the passengers, gazing around.

"Look at the view!" cried the lady in blue.

"It's a long, long way down!" called the boy with the buckets.

"Don't lean out!" yelled his mother and father.

"I just can't look…" worried the Little Train as he rattled over the bridge.

And when he did open his eyes…

"Ooooooh!" called the passengers as they whizzed into the tunnel.

"Ooooooh!" echoed the tunnel as the Little Train rushed through.

And in just a few minutes, they were all safely through the tunnel.

"Phewwwwwwww!" yelled the passengers, looking around.

"Where are my sunglasses?" cried the lady in blue.

"I've dropped my ticket!" shouted the boy with the buckets.

"Oh no, not again!" groaned his mother and father.

"I'm, I'm, I'm... beginning to like this!" chuffed the cheerful Little Train.

But ahead on the line stood something large and lazy.

"Hold on to your seats everyone!" shrieked the Little Train.

"Shooooo!" cried the passengers.

"Moooooo!" said the cow as the Little Train rushed towards her.

"Get off the line!" barked the man with the beard.

"I, I, I… can't s-s-s-stop!"
screeched the Little Train, braking
as hard as any train could.

But just as it seemed that disaster was near, the cow leapt away and at last the track was clear.

"Hoooooooraaaaaaaay!" called the passengers, chuckling and cheering.

"Phew, phew, phew, phew... is there much farther to go?" sighed the Little Train, beginning to run out of steam.

But round the next bend was the end of the line!

"The seeeeeeeeeea!" cheered the passengers, smiling and waving.

"Nearly, nearly, nearly… there,"
sighed the tired Little Train, as the
passengers jostled and jiggled and
giggled on their way to the sea.

"Goodbyeeeeeeeeeee!" called the passengers, leaving the station.

"We'll see you later!" called the terrible twins, swinging their spades in a dangerous way!

"What time do we leave?" laughed the lady in blue.

"At six o'clock sharp," said the smart Station Mistress. "You'll be rested by then, won't you, Little Train?"

"Yes!" The brave Little Train gave a sigh and a smile. And happily dreaming of making great journeys, he soon fell asleep to the sounds of the sea.